"HOW MUCH FUN ARE YOU GETTING OUT OF LIFE?"

NAGAI KAFŪ
Born 1879, Tokyo
Died 1959, Ichikawa

UNO KŌJI
Born 1891, Fukuoka
Died 1961, Tokyo

AKUTAGAWA RYŪNOSUKE
Born 1892, Tokyo
Died 1927, Tokyo

These three stories are from the forthcoming *Penguin Book of Japanese Short Stories*.

AKUTAGAWA IN PENGUIN MODERN CLASSICS
Rashōmon and Seventeen Other Stories

Three Japanese Short Stories

Translated by Jay Rubin

PENGUIN BOOKS

PENGUIN CLASSICS

UK | USA | Canada | Ireland | Australia
India | New Zealand | South Africa

Penguin Books is part of the Penguin Random House group
of companies whose addresses can be found at
global.penguinrandomhouse.com.

Penguin
Random House
UK

This selection first published 2018

012

Translation copyright © Jay Rubin, 2018

Set in 11.2/13.75 pt Dante MT Std
Typeset by Jouve (UK), Milton Keynes
Printed and bound in Great Britain by Clays Ltd, Elcograf S.p.A.

ISBN: 978-0-241-33974-9

www.greenpenguin.co.uk

MIX
Paper from
responsible sources
FSC® C018179

Penguin Random House is committed to a
sustainable future for our business, our readers
and our planet. This book is made from Forest
Stewardship Council® certified paper.

Contents

Behind the Prison
by Nagai Kafū

My dearest Excellency,

Thank you for your letter. I have been back in Japan for nearly five months.

I was in the West, as you know, but I was unable to find any fixed employment or to earn academic credentials during my time there. All I brought home with me was my collection of concert, opera and theatre programmes, as well as my photographs and nude paintings of female entertainers. I am a full thirty years old now, but, far from being prepared to start my own family, I continue to while away my days in a single room on my father's estate, which is located behind the prison in Ichigaya. It has a rather imposing gate and a lush growth of tall trees. I'm sure you could find it easily just by asking for my father.

I will probably be here, doing nothing, for the time being. Indeed, I may have to spend the rest of my life like this. Not that I am surprised to find myself in this situation. The question of what I should do once I returned to Japan is the same old one that continued to trouble me even while I was lost in music or intoxicated by the lips of a lover, or gazing at the Seine in the evening from the shelter of spring leaves. I confess it was my inability to solve this painful problem, and not any irrepressible longing for art, that enabled a weakling like me to bear the loneliness of living abroad for such a long time. In a foreign country, so long as one's health is unimpaired, one need have no fear of starving. One can abandon all concern for reputation and answer newspaper advertisements to become a waiter, a shop assistant – anything at all. Without the hypocritical label of 'gentleman', one no longer feels the shameful need to deceive others. One gains opportunities to observe the hidden truths of society and to touch the genuine tears of life. Oh, but once one has returned to the land of one's birth – there is no place more constricting – one's surroundings no longer permit such freedom, and one can no longer simply transcend the demands of social position. Like a skiff on a fog-shrouded ocean, I had no clear way ahead of me, no plans for the future when I landed in the port of Kobe with its low shingled houses and its monstrously twisted black pines. Perhaps I could stay there in hiding, I thought, rather than return to Tokyo where so many people knew me. At that very moment, a heartfelt cry reached my ears, the deep, strong voice of someone ascending the crowded gangplank –

'Welcome back, brother!'

And who should appear before me, dressed in a university student uniform, but my very own younger brother! I had naturally lost touch with my father, especially during the past two or three years, but, greatly worried, he had contacted the steamship company, learned which vessel I had boarded and sent my brother to meet the ship.

Shamed by the extent of my father's efforts, I felt an instinctive urge to hide my face. At the same time, I was sick of parental affection. Why did my parents not simply turn their backs on a son who had proved himself so unfilial? And why did that son feel so threatened by his sense of gratitude towards his parents? Why, when he tried to force himself not to feel such gratitude, did he succeed only in filling himself with pain and dread? No, nothing in this world is as oppressive and debilitating as blood ties. Any other relationship – be it with friend, lover, wife; be it obligatory or constraining or difficult – is something one has consciously entered into at some point. Only one's ties with parents and siblings are formed at birth and are unbreakable. And even if one succeeds in severing such relationships, all one is left with is the unbearable agony of conscience. It is simply one's destiny. Your Excellency, I am certain you have seen sparrows that have built nests in the eaves of your home. No sooner do the young fly away from the nest than they escape forever from this fateful shadow. Nor do the parents make any attempt to bind their offspring's hearts with morality.

One glance at my brother, born of the same blood, his face so resembling my own, was all it took to fill me with an indescribably cruel emotion. In an instant, it seemed to sweep away the inexpressible nostalgia I felt, along with the sorrow, the joy, the vivid sense of freedom of my wandering years, leaving nothing behind. Suddenly the air enveloping me seemed to grow still, as might be imagined in a medieval monastery, cold as ice and clear as a mirror.

'The six o'clock is an express train,' my brother said. 'Let's buy our tickets.'

I said nothing in reply. At Kobe Station all I did was stare at a few unrefined but voluptuous American girls buying bouquets from a flower vendor. After arriving at Shinbashi Station the next morning, I found myself being whisked by rickshaw to my father's estate behind the Ichigaya prison.

They held a little banquet for me at home that evening. My father turns sixty this year. He probably felt he had to give the party to keep up appearances regarding his son and heir, whatever the truth of the situation. They put me in the seat of honour before the *tokonoma* alcove where a calligraphic scroll hung inscribed with a long string of Chinese characters that meant nothing to me. Sitting at the other end of the table were my mother and father. To my right was the brother who had been chosen to carry on my mother's family as pastor of a small church. To my left was my parents' youngest child, the brother who had met my ship, sitting there in his impressive uniform, its gold buttons gleaming. There were flecks of grey in my father's moustache, but his tanned face was more radiant than ever, and the added years only seemed to increase the youthfulness of his robust frame. My mother, by contrast, looked as though she had aged ten or twenty years during my absence. Now she was just a shrivelled-up little old lady I could hardly recognize.

I would want a wife or lover and, I dare say, my mother to remain eternally young and beautiful. When I saw her looking so aged, I could hardly lift my chopsticks to join in the feasting. Sorrow, pity and a mix of even stronger emotions struck me all at once: an intense desire to revolt against the fate that dooms us to perish.

Your Excellency, my mother was a young woman until I left for the West. People who didn't know us very well used to ask if she was my sister. She was born in old Edo and raised to be a great lover of the kabuki theatre, a skilled singer of *nagauta* ballads while accompanying herself on the shamisen. She also played the koto. Approaching forty, she could still sing that wonderful passage from 'Azuma Hakkei' with ease, the shamisen tuned up to the high *roppon* scale: 'Pine needle pins in her hair, she makes her way along the dewy cobblestones beside the Sumida River, writing brush in its case wet with ink . . .' And yet she was very restrained in her tastes. As far back as her teenage years she is said to have hated the colour red, and I never saw an under-kimono of hers that could be described as gaudy, even when the family's clothing was spread out to dry at the height of summer: perhaps a muted persimmon-coloured grid pattern, or a pale blue Yūzen print of plovers against white-capped waves. I'll never forget all the theatres she took me to in the arms of my wet nurse – the Hisamatsu-za, the Shintomi-za, the Chitose-za – where we would indulge in a rare treat of broiled eel on rice in our box seats. And those marvellous winter days in the warmth of the *kotatsu*, where she would spread out her colourful woodblock prints of such legendary actors as Hikosa and Tanosuke and tell me all about the old days in the theatre! Oh, the cruelty of time that destroys all things! If only I could stay for ever and ever with my mother, Your

Excellency, enjoying those magnificent pastimes! For her I would gladly ferry across the Sumida on the coldest winter day to buy her those *sakura-mochi* sweets from old Edo that she loved so much. But medicine? That is another matter. Not even on the warmest day would I want to go buy her medicine.

Never have I had it in me to surrender to those ancient articles of faith which mankind has been commanded to follow. Such precepts are too cruel, too cold. Rather than bow before them, how often have I cried out in anguish, wishing that 'I' and 'the precepts' could be united in a perfect, warm embrace! But having despaired of such an easy resolution, I determined that I would confront them head-on, that I would do battle with Heaven's retribution. My father is a stern disciplinarian, a diligent man, a fierce enemy of all that is evil. The day after I came home, he quietly asked me about my plans for the future. He wanted to know how I intended to preserve my honour as a man, to fulfil my duty as a citizen of the empire.

Should I become a language teacher? No, I could never presume to present myself as a teacher of French. Any Frenchman would know the language far better than I could ever hope to.

Should I become a newspaper reporter? No, I can

imagine myself becoming a thief some day, but I am not so inured to vice that I would treat justice and morality as merchandise the way such people do. The scandal sheets *Yorozu chōhō* and *Niroku shinpō* present themselves as paragons of virtue, but any society reformed by them would be far darker than a society left wholly unreformed. I worry too much about this to sink to their level.

Should I become a magazine reporter? No, I am not losing sleep over social progress or human happiness to the point where I would stand up as an advocate for good causes. Nor am I the least bit bothered, as some journalists seem to be, by the cannibalistic, incestuous lives of animals.

Should I become an artist? No, this is Japan, not the West. Far from demanding art, Japanese society looks upon it as a nuisance. The state has established a system of education by intimidation and forces us to produce grotesque vocalizations that no member of the Yamato race has ever pronounced – T, V, D, F – and if you can't say them you have no right to exist in Meiji society. They do this primarily so that some day we will invent a new torpedo or gun, certainly not to have us intone the poems of Verlaine or Mallarmé – and still less to have us sing the 'Marseillaise' or the 'Internationale', with their messages of revolution and pacifism. Those of us with a deep-seated desire to devote ourselves to the Muses or to Venus must leave this fatherland of ours with all its stringent rules before we can begin to embrace our harps. This would be of the greatest benefit both to the nation and to art itself.

No, no, there is not a single profession in this world that will keep me alive for the days that remain to me. Should I become a rickshaw puller wandering the streets of the city? No, I have too great a sense of responsibility for that. Could I safely fulfil the demands of the profession by delivering my passengers uninjured to their destinations? And what if I became a manservant cooking rice? Mixed in with the countless grains, might there not be an invisible chip of stone that would tear my master's stomach, endangering his life? The more precise and subtle a human being's awareness, the less he can presume to take on any profession, however humble. First he must starve, he must freeze, he must numb the precision of his mind, he must be blinded by his own selfish desires. At the very least, he must ignore the teachings of the ancient sages. Oh, you who sing of how hard it is to make a living! How I envy you!

I turned to my father and said, 'There is nothing for me to do in this world. Please think of me as mad or crippled, and do not press me to live up to normal worldly expectations.'

For his part, my father would have found it a stain on the family honour were his son to become known as a reporter or a clerk or a servant or some other lowly worker. 'Fortunately we have a spare room,' he said, 'and food. You can just live here quietly and keep to yourself.' With that, he brought the discussion to a close.

These past few months, I have spent one blank day after another gazing out at the garden. The hot August sunlight casts the shadows of the luxuriant trees over the garden's broad expanse of green moss. Here and there patches of light break through the trees' black shadows, trembling with each passing breeze. I find the sight inexpressibly beautiful. A cicada cries. A crow caws. And yet the world, exhausted by the scorching heat, is as hushed as at night. A sudden shower strikes, but because the larger part of the sky remains blue and clear, I can see each thick thread of rain falling in the bright light. Each of the plants responds differently to the downpour, the delicate ones bowing to earth, the stronger ones springing upwards, the sound of the raindrops striking them varying from light to heavy depending on the thickness of their leaves. The shower symphony rises to a great crescendo with the rumbling bass drum of thunder that rolls through, to be followed by the gentle moderato of the green frogs' flutes and a final hush as sudden as the piece's opening. Then the entire garden – from the tiniest tree branches soaring aloft to the leaf tips of the *kumazasa* bamboo creeping among the ornamental boulders – is strung with crystalline jewels that lend a startling radiance to the mossy carpet, across which the massed trees' long, diagonal, cloud-like shadows drift until the evening cicadas call and twilight arrives. Around the time a wind chime begins ringing incessantly and the servants light our paper lanterns, from the street beyond the front gate comes the light clip-clop of wooden clogs and the laughter of young women. A student ambles along, chanting a poem, a harmonica sounds, and somewhere far away the pop of what must be fireworks. A street musician passes by, lamenting another broken heart to the twang of a shamisen. The night deepens . . .

The insect cries grow louder with each passing day. When I lie down to sleep at night, a terrifying din travels from the closed-off garden all the way to the space beneath the veranda outside my room. What power rules these tens of thousands of creatures, what makes them all unite in one voice to besiege me like this? I feel as if I am camped alone on a magnificent plain beneath an endless sky, waiting an eternity for the dawn to break, but when I open my eyes the dim lamp on my desk reveals that I am actually lying beneath a low board ceiling that might come crashing down at any moment, my body confined by suffocating colourless walls and blank sliding paper doors. Then a keen sense of the nature of life in Japan overwhelms me – so limited, so lacking in depth. The sudden clatter of raindrops against the ceiling sounds like someone trying to play a broken koto. I hear the night wind tearing through the trees above. But the sound lacks the depth of a lion's roaring in a dark valley, and I wonder if what I hear is the rustling of reeds on the shoreline of a great river flowing through a tropical plain. The insects cry without cease. They cry even after the break of dawn and the arrival of noon. And that is not all I hear. The rains fall day after day.

What a humid climate we have! I try closing all the shoji and lighting the hibachi in the corner of the room, but my kimono is still so moist I can't help wondering if my skin will grow scales like some fishy creature's. The fine leather binding of *The Diary of Countess Krasinska*, given to me as a keepsake by Rosalyn when I left America, has been all but destroyed by mould. The lacquer shoes in which I danced with Yvonne in a Parisian ball-room have grown a ghostly white fur. Cruel stains have formed on the summer topcoat I spread on the grass when lying there with Hélène in the Bois de Boulogne.

I hear the sad calls of vendors wandering through the neighbourhood and the clatter of shutters being closed nearby as night falls. Oh, the nights in Japan! No words can describe their darkness! Darker than death, darker than the grave, cold, lonely. Shall I call it a wall of darkness – an indestructible barrier that cannot be pierced by any blade of rage or despair, that cannot be scorched by any flame of rancour or frenzy? I sit beneath the only spot of light in the whole room, a single oil lamp, reading and rereading the letters I exchanged with the people I knew in those days of joy, unable to read a letter to the end before having to press my face, in tears, against its pages. The cries of the insects fill the garden.

Eventually, however, it dawns on me that the intense cries of the insects have begun slowly to fade with the passing of each dark and lonely night. I find myself wearing a new padded *haori* over my lined kimono, the smell of the freshly dyed cloth oddly sickening to inhale. The rains have ceased. In contrast to the morning and evening chill, the sunny afternoons are frighteningly hot. The leaves have turned yellow, but how strange to watch them as they flutter down through the windless air on to the garden's mossy carpet in the harsh, summer-like sunlight. I feel the deep melancholy of the French poet who sang of the South American climate: 'Here the leaves scatter in the April spring.'

I go out to the garden one afternoon, a partially

read book of poems in hand, and walk among the beds. The streaming rays illuminate each overlapping leaf of the plums, the maples, the other trees that grow in such profusion, casting their shadows like patterns on the mossy ground. Deep in this shade stands a gazebo. Beyond it is an unobstructed view of a flowering field. I sit to take in the immense blue sky at a glance. Thin white clouds spread across the blue from west to east as if painted with a brush, never moving however long I gaze at them. Countless dragonflies flit back and forth like the swallows one sees high in the summer skies of France. Multicoloured cosmos, taller than the gazebo, bloom in profusion beneath the harsh sun, spreading to all corners of the field, each of which is densely covered in low-growing *kumazasa* bamboo. Crimson amaranths seem to burst into flame. The Chinese bellflowers and asters retain their brilliant purple, but the white-flowered bush clovers are already past their peak and bow to the ground like the dishevelled tresses of a woman who has thrown herself down in tears, flowing towards my feet upon the gazebo's paving stones. In their dewy shadows, one or two surviving insects cry out in thin melodic strains.

Ah, this blue sky, this sunlight: mementos of a forgotten summer. How could one imagine it to be October, to be autumn? The barest hint of a breeze turns the pages of the poetry book on my knees until I have a clear view of the final stanza of Baudelaire's sad 'Song of Autumn':

> *Ah! laissez-moi, mon front posé sur vos genoux,*
> *Goûter, en regrettant l'été blanc et torride,*
> *De l'arrière saison le rayon jaune et doux!*

'Ah! let me, with my head bowed on your knees, / Taste the sweet, yellow rays of the end of autumn, / While I mourn for the white, torrid summer!'

No matter what I see, even the most beautiful flower, I wonder if it is blooming only to make us think of the sadness to come when it has withered and died. The delightful intoxication of love, I can only believe, exists to give us a taste of the sadness to come after parting. And surely the autumn sunlight shines this beautifully in order to tell us, 'Know ye that the sadness of winter will be here tomorrow.' Now and then I become strangely agitated and, wishing to see the fading sunlight for even a few seconds longer, I leave to walk not just in the garden but through the gate and into the streets beyond. Ah, what scenes the autumn sun – the autumn sun of my birthplace – has shown me!

As I said at the beginning of this letter, my home is located behind the Ichigaya prison. When I began my travels nearly six years ago, this was a tranquil patch of countryside. 'You know,' I would tell the city girls, 'it's that place where the azaleas bloom.' Only then would it dawn on them which area I was talking about. Now, however, it is just another new district slapped together on the edge of Tokyo. All that is unchanged are the long prison embankment that looms over the narrow street and the life of the poor who toil here beneath it.

The first thing you see across from our front gate is the long, weather-beaten wooden fence enclosing the jailers' compound and then the horrible embankment itself, casting a shadow over the narrow street and topped by a spiky hedge, beneath which not even a weasel could burrow. The flanks of the embankment are covered by a prickly growth of frightful devil's thistle, one touch of which would cause your hand to swell in pain. On stormy September days, I would expect the wind to blow over the dilapidated fence around the jailers' compound, and, sure enough, the next morning, when the street was littered with tree branches, I would see pairs of prisoners chained together at the waist in orange jackets with numbers on their collars and wearing bamboo coolie hats, pulling up and repairing the fence under the supervision of uniformed, sword-bearing guards. Sometimes, too, at the height of summer, a gang of prisoners would mow the weeds on the embankment. Passers-by would stop and stare at them in silence, eyes filled with simultaneous loathing and curiosity.

The embankment runs in a long, straight line from both left and right until it curves sharply inwards at the centre, where it ends in a large black gate between two thick columns. The gate's heavy-looking doors are always tightly shut. No voices can be heard from the other side of the gate, and there is nothing to be seen from the outside except a narrow chimney poking up above a low tiled roof, and four or five skinny cedars. The trees stand some distance away from one another, which to my eyes suggests that even these unfeeling plants are being kept apart in the prison yard to prevent them from whispering together, plotting evil schemes under cover of darkness.

Where the raised embankment suddenly gives out some distance from the gate, the narrow street becomes a downward-winding slope, on one side of which, during my absence, some rich gentleman seems to have built a new residence upon high stone walls, while on the other side the road is lined with the same kind of rental tenement houses that have been there for ever, like a row of boxes, one atop another, going down the hill. The prison embankment stands behind them like a blank wall, thanks to which no ray of sunlight has ever reached the tenements. Their wooden foundations are rotting and overgrown with moss, and insects have eaten holes through the bottom edges of the storm shutters standing outside each unit's front lattice door during the day. Two or three of the units invariably have barely legible 'For Rent' signs hanging from them. And always there are signs soliciting piecework. Often when passing these tenements on a cold winter evening, I have seen on a small window's torn, soot-smeared shoji the pale shadow cast by an oil lamp of a woman with tousled locks retying her obi. And on sultry summer evenings, peering through sparse reed blinds, I have had a clear view of the secrets of these people's households. How well I recall passing by here on afternoons when the prisoners' used bath water would gush down the drainage ditches below the tenements' windows, raising clouds of foul-smelling steam. It must be the same even now. Most shocking of all were the local housewives with scabrous babies on their backs, seizing the opportunity to make use of the hot water on cold, clear days, to wash things in the ditches as they chattered away with mouthfuls of crooked teeth, or in summertime scattering the stinking water on the road.

Shabby shops line both sides of the road at the bottom of the hill – a sweet shop, a hardware store, a tobacconist, a greengrocer, a firewood seller – among which a rice merchant and soy sauce dealer are the only good old-fashioned establishments with thick pillars that might arouse vague feelings of rebellion. Which is not to suggest a modern socialist reaction on my part, but merely a fantasy inspired by the traditional look of the houses and starring such popular stage heroes as Jiraiya or Nezumi Kozō. Oddly, there are two old stonemasons down here, and especially noticeable of late has been the increase in the number of home-delivery tempura shops and fishmongers, proof of the day-by-day increase in the number of tenements in the area. Upon a wooden counter disturbingly overgrown with green moss sits a shallow, round wooden sushi rice mixing bowl half filled with greasy water containing fish parts, shaved fish meat and rows of skewered shellfish that have been dried in the sun, almost all bearing price tags of ten sen or less. As far as I can see, the eyes of the dead fish are all stagnant and cloudy, the scales on their bellies have faded to a pale bluish white, and the chilled bloody edges of their sliced meat have lost so much of their freshness that the colours in each shop front are not only unpleasant but downright depressing. The sight of dripping blood used to terrify me whenever I passed a butcher's shop in the West, but here, to the contrary, the thought that this faded, cold fish meat is the only source of nourishment for the blood of most of my countrymen fills me with an inexpressible sorrow. All the more so when

I turn the corner at the bottom of the hill near sundown and hear the hoarse voice of the old man at a stand there displaying nothing but fish bones and guts with a scarf tied over the top of his head and yelling, 'Get your *tai* guts cheap! Get your *tai* guts cheap!' He's surrounded by housewives with babies on their backs, the women all screaming at him to bring his prices even lower.

Above the sand-whitened tiled roofs, the evening sky's great expanse glows less red than a murky burnt sienna because autumn is nearing its end, casting shadows more intensely black than the dark of night. The narrow road is suddenly crowded with men most likely coming home from work – rather well-dressed gentlemen, military men on horseback, passengers in rickshaws. All move as black shadows, without a single light to be seen in the houses on either side of the road. Running with dizzying speed among them are children at play, waving sticks and other playthings. I have seen men in Western suits stop at the fish guts stand by the roadside on their way home from the office before climbing the hill towards the back of the prison, carrying their purchases wrapped in bamboo sheathing. The sight brings to mind scenes of dinner in poor Japanese households.

The lattice door of a tenement unit clatters but shows no sign of opening, nor does the patched grey shoji behind it catch any lamplight from within. The threshold remains in darkness. One Western-suited gentleman steps out of his never-polished rubber-soled shoes, opens the shoji and steps inside to find his disabled old mother coughing beneath the window of the tiny three-mat room. The baby is squealing. Shocked to realize that night has fallen, the wife squats down like a frog on the kitchen floor, nervously trying to fill the lamp with oil. Alerted to her husband's homecoming by the sound of the opening door, she turns her colourless face towards him in the sky-light's afterglow, loose hairs from her dry-looking bun floating off in all directions. Though not cold, she sniffles as she offers him a blank 'Welcome home'.

Instead of answering, the husband asks, 'You're only getting to the lamp now?' and he scolds her for her poor housekeeping. His old mother crawls out of her bedding on the floor and tries to intervene. Whichever side she takes, the results are the same and the argument blossoms. Just then the eight-year-old comes in wailing about the fight that sent him flying into the drainage ditch, and he has the mud-smeared kimono to prove it. Now the argument centres on him until the evening dishes line up beneath the dusky lamp – boiled beans, pickled vegetables, a stew of fish bones and scallions, and a rice tub smeared with dirty fingerprints. Gathered around their flimsy table, the family talk about uncle so-and-so, who showed up this afternoon wanting to know the cost of

Mother's medicine in the spring. They talk about how the wife's father lost his job. They talk about their everyday expenses. The family's mouths were formed for only two purposes: to eat food and to complain endlessly about the hardships of life. Whether they are impoverished or not, it amounts to the same thing. The pure art of conversation for its own sake is lost on people like this. They have no need of language for anything other than seeking advice, complaining, harping on the same old stories and quarrelling.

Such are the scenes that have greeted me when I have strolled out of our front gate and up the road behind the prison in the hope of enjoying the autumn light. What grips my heart still more painfully are the tragic acts of animal cruelty I see on the road. Two or three freight wagons in a row drawn by emaciated horses over long distances, some loaded with bales of rice, others with lumber or bricks or other heavy payloads, will be led through the rear gate of the prison at the top of the slope. Unfortunately for the animals, the open area in front of the gate rises at the same angle as the road itself, which causes the wheels of the turning wagons to dig into the soft, damp soil, and this makes it impossible for the exhausted horses to drag the wagons up and through the gate in a single effort. When this happens, the rough

teamsters scream at the horses and beat them merci-
lessly with fallen branches. The men yank violently on
the reins, and the horses clamp their white teeth on the
bits in what seems like unbearable pain. Their manes
bristle, their bloodshot eyes bulge and finally their fore-
legs collapse, bringing them down on the gravel surface.
Everything on the narrow slope comes to a halt whenever this occurs, but far from being shocked, most
passers-by stare open-mouthed in amusement. Here,
then, is proof that cruelty to animals is an issue only to
a few Christians, not a pressing problem for the whole
of Japanese society. Is this a matter for grief or celebra-
tion? Witnessing these scenes only deepens my sense
that the Japanese are a warlike people who are sure to
defeat the Russians once again in the future. Oh, pat-
riots, set your minds at ease. As long as you can make a
yellow man like me believe in the white man's Yellow
Peril, you should feel free to go on cursing your wives,
oppressing your children and giving three cheers for the
empire with glasses held high. And so we declare: the
age is still too young for us to worry that melancholy
poets will begin giving voice to their ideals.

Slowly, gradually, I have come to avoid and even fear
the prospect of venturing beyond the front gate. Yes, let
me gaze in quiet solitude at the shifting autumn sunlight
through the glass doors of my veranda.

Sadly, autumn is already beginning to fade. The intense sunlight that made the afternoons seem like summer has weakened now, and the sky is always thickly overcast. It looks like the frosted glass skylight of a large atelier, across which cloud curtains move, sending down pale refracted rays as soft as twilight. Shadows and colours seen in this light seem to have a transparent clarity that cannot be sensed in the blinding glare of the sun. The trees have lost their leaves, their crowns bare and bright, their slender black branches tracing innumerable upward-thrusting lines against the sky. Behind them, the gazebo's thatched roof and the field's withered grasses glow yellow through the black evergreens in the distance. Half hidden by the ornamental stones beyond the veranda, tiny golden chrysanthemums bloom like stars. From there to the far end of the garden spreads an unbroken velvet carpet of moss even more lustrous than in summer. Two or three wagtails, pecking at the tiny moss flowers, move across the carpet, flicking their long, pointed tails up and down. How sharply their grey feathers and the crimson leaves of the dwarf sumac bonsai upon a boulder contrast with the broad green lustre of the moss!

No wind blows. The shifting, cloudy autumn afternoon maintains its thick silence, giving the illusion that the outlines of objects have been obliterated, leaving only their colours. On occasion, a few remaining leaves will suddenly flutter down from a tree. This unexpected stirring of the air is like the deep sigh of some mysterious creature. When that happens, every single leaf in the garden – from the evergreens' lush needles to the clumps of chrysanthemums among the stones – resounds with an inexpressible sorrow and then, a moment later, reverts to silence. Atop the smooth moss: the wagtails again, the chrysanthemum blossoms, the bonsai's crimson foliage. Ah, the light of a dream, the thin overcast of departing autumn.

Excellency! Since yesterday I have been reading Verlaine's book of prison verse *Sagesse*:

> O my God, you have wounded me with love.
> The wound remains open, unhealed.
> O my God, you have wounded me with love . . .

Excellency! Please come visit me once before the onset of winter. I am lonely.

Closet LLB
by Uno Kōji

Five years have gone by since Otsukotsu Sansaku received his Bachelor of Laws degree from the university and became known as Otsukotsu Sansaku, LLB, but he still has no fixed occupation. Almost nine years have gone by since he first arrived in Tokyo from the provinces, but he still spreads his bedding in the same room of the same boarding house he chose at the beginning (while ownership of the boarding house itself has changed hands thirteen times).

As an undergraduate, Sansaku was, in fact, present on at least two-thirds of the days his college was open for classes – perhaps because the rules prohibited anything less – and his grades were on the high side. At university, however, he averaged ten days a year, passing through the campus gate no more than forty times in four years, as a result of which he graduated second from the bottom in his class.

Back in the third or fourth year of primary school,

Sansaku became obsessed with boys' magazines and fairy tales, and he aspired, if somewhat vaguely, to become a children's author like Iwaya Sazanami.

His father died when Sansaku was three, leaving Sansaku and his mother enough money to live on for the rest of their lives. His mother took the extra precaution of entrusting the property to an influential relative, but this had the reverse effect of plunging them into misfortune when, unexpectedly, the relative went bankrupt, losing not only his own property but theirs as well. This happened the year Sansaku entered middle school.

At that point another relative, a man named Ōike, stepped forward to pay his school fees. Ōike was a cousin of Sansaku's father whom the father had aided monetarily and in other ways and who, unexpectedly, had succeeded in business and become a millionaire. When the fourteen-year-old Sansaku finished his first year of middle school, Ōike brought him to live in the Ōike household and insisted that he take an examination to transfer into a prestigious business school. Try as he might, Sansaku could not make himself study for the exam, and two days before the appointed date he ran away from the Ōikes' to his own house (or, rather, to the house of his mother's parents, who had taken them in after the bankruptcy).

Ōike then gave up on his plans for Sansaku and

resigned himself to paying the boy's tuition and letting him continue through the full five years of middle school. Sansaku had had excellent grades all the way through primary and middle school, which is not to say that he was working especially hard in middle school. Far from it. Indeed, he was already completely immersed in magazines and fiction. But the ambition Iwaya Sazanami had sparked in his earliest years had been evolving bit by bit: first, Sansaku found himself wanting to be a staff writer at a magazine, and then, from the third year of middle school, he embraced the unshakeable goal of becoming a novelist. To this very day, that has not changed. Which only goes to prove that we are dealing here with someone who was once a childhood prodigy.

Yet another problem arose when Sansaku graduated from middle school at the age of eighteen. Ōike, convinced that this was the time for him to take action, again pressed Sansaku to study business, but Sansaku insisted that his future lay in literature. The two clashed repeatedly until it was decided (through the offices of a third party) that Sansaku should take the middle path and study law at college. Not even the gifted Otsukotsu Sansaku was able to grasp exactly how law was the 'middle path' between business and literature, but he did see that any further resistance to the wishes of the relative who was paying for his education would be both futile and against his better interests, and in the end he resigned himself to entering the college's pre-law programme. Thus it came about that, through the three years of college and four more at university, Sansaku steeped himself exclusively in literature while supposedly settled in law. He managed to squeeze through his university law exams at least, and five years ago became, if in name only, a Bachelor of Laws: Otsukotsu Sansaku, LLB.

Just about the time he graduated from university, Ōike died. This did not spell the end of the Ōike line, however, since Mr Ōike had a perfectly fine heir to carry on his name. But the payments to Sansaku came to a halt the moment he graduated, almost as if Ōike's debt to Sansaku's father had now been settled once and for all. As noted earlier, Sansaku is a Bachelor of Laws, but he knows almost nothing about the law. Not one of his relatives, who felt only antipathy towards him, offered to help him find employment. Nor did he, in his strange arrogance, bother to approach any of his senior law colleagues in search of an opening. None of them liked Sansaku, either.

In this way did our poor Bachelor of Laws suddenly find himself pressed to make ends meet. While at university, most of his friends had been in the literature department rather than law, and it was through those friends that Sansaku was able to live from one poverty-stricken day to the next by doing the occasional cut-rate translation or writing fairy tales, though even so he has run up a sizable debt at his boarding house. In addition, once he graduated he found that he was expected to send fifteen yen every month to his elderly mother in the country.

Over the past year or two, Sansaku has fallen into ever-deepening poverty. There has never been enough translation work, and he has run out of ideas for fairy tales. Still, visiting literary friends to beg for work has been just as hard for him as calling upon his senior colleagues in law. (In other words, though arrogant, he is also a man of great diffidence.) Before he knew it, then, his payments to his mother fell further and further behind. Once that happened, it ceased to bother him, and he gradually stopped sending anything at all. In the end, he could toss her urgent letters aside with hardly a twinge of conscience.

Then, just a month ago, a letter arrived from the country. As we have seen, Sansaku might allow two or three days to go by before reading his mother's letters, and some he never read at all; but this one, fortunately, he opened and read immediately – 'fortunately' because it brought him excellent news. Since he had so often been late sending money to her, his mother said, their relatives had begun to hear of her difficulties, and several of them who, like Ōike, had been aided by Sansaku's late father and had since done especially well for themselves, had got together and collected ten thousand yen, enabling her to open a small but dependable shop.

This news brought Sansaku such a tremendous sense of relief from the cares of day-to-day living that he felt quite drained.

'What was that again?' he muttered to himself, recalling the last part of his mother's letter. ' "Our relatives say they pooled their resources and helped me open a shop because you have failed to support me the way you ought to, Sansaku, so under no circumstances should you even *dream* of pestering your mother" – "not that we are in a position to say such a thing," said the hypocritical bastards! – "for a loan." A loan? Who the hell's asking for a loan? But wait a minute,' he went on, trying to make sense of the situation. 'If they gave it to her, it's hers. And besides, it's not as if I'm some prodigal son planning to "pester" his mother for money to support his dissolute lifestyle. This will be my chance to sit down and do some serious work. Which means . . . and so . . .

'All right, then, let me just set all thought of money aside and take the time to apply myself to a grown-up novel.' (Having written so many fairy tales over the years, this is how Sansaku refers to standard novels.)

'Because I've had to send out fifteen yen or so every

month until now, I've been compelled to keep taking stupid jobs I absolutely detested, but now that my mother's livelihood is assured . . .'

No sooner had his thoughts brought him this far than Sansaku felt that sudden, draining sense of relief, like a traveller who remains unconscious of his fatigue as long as he keeps hurrying down the road but who collapses in a heap from exhaustion the moment he realizes he has reached his destination (though in fact, as stated earlier, Sansaku had by no means been making regular monthly remittances to his mother). Once he felt it was no longer necessary for him to act, the will to act simply vanished. Although he did at least feel an occasional urge to write a grown-up novel – after all, it was an ambition he had often harboured to the point of ignoring everything else, including his studies for a time – it occurred to him that, even if he managed to finish one, far from earning him easy money like his fairy tales, just getting it accepted would require enormous effort on his part. And so he flung his pen away.

Every single day since then he has spent either visiting with friends or sleeping. Sansaku's style of sleeping deserves special mention. His small tatami-matted room has the standard tall, deep closet divided by a sturdy shelf into upper and lower compartments for storing his futon and covers behind a pair of sliding paper doors, but

Sansaku long ago decided that it was too much trouble to open the closet door and pull the bedding out every day to spread it on the tatami. Instead he cleared out the upper compartment and now keeps his futon spread out permanently on the shelf. He sleeps in the closet with the doors open and never has to make his bed.

'This is it! This is the answer!' he cried in delight at his own discovery. 'I may have been born in the sticks, but I'm different from the typical farmer or merchant's son. I'm delicately built, so I can't sleep just anywhere with a pile of magazines or a folded cushion for a pillow. This is it!'

Lazy as he was, Sansaku still managed to wake up early every morning, wash his face and eat breakfast. After an hour or two, however, he would crawl back into his bed on the closet shelf. Usually he would be awakened by the maid when she brought his lunch on a tray, which she would set on the tatami. He would slip down from the shelf, sit cross-legged on the floor to finish his lunch and then immediately burrow his way back into the bedding on the closet shelf. Then, in the evening, he would be awakened yet again by the maid when she arrived with his dinner on the usual tray. While he slept, of course, Sansaku was unconscious, so it seemed as if his three meals – breakfast, lunch and dinner – were delivered to him in rapid succession the way a waiter in a Western restaurant brings one dish after another to the table. He spent most evenings strolling around the city or visiting friends to talk about nothing in particular. Bedtime was two o'clock in the morning for him most days. Still, it was Sansaku more than anyone who was amazed at how much he could sleep.

'On the other hand, I never sleep without dreaming,' he would often think to himself. 'Which may mean that the amount of time I am actually asleep is short. If ordinary people dream a little while sleeping, in my case it's more that I sleep a little while dreaming.'

Now, the boarding house in which Otsukotsu Sansaku, LLB, lives is halfway up a hill, and it stands on a plot of land that is two feet lower than the street level, as a result of which, even though his room is on the second floor facing the street (that is, the hill), the faces of people passing by are at virtually the same height as his when he is sitting on his tatami floor. This means that when he leaves his window open and keeps the door of his closet slid back, he can lie amid the bedding on his closet shelf, watching the street and closely observing the passers-by – none of whom, of course, can imagine that there is a person in the closet watching them and who must consequently pass by unconcerned about what they assume to be an empty room.

This way, from among the folds of his bedding,

Sansaku can spend certain intervals – the five or ten minutes between the time his eyes have tired of reading magazines and the time he drifts into his morning or afternoon nap – watching the people climbing or descending the hill as if he were seeing them in a play. He has developed the ability to pick out local residents even if he has never spoken a word to them, saying to himself, 'Aha! That's so-and-so from such-and-such a house.' Quite often, while lying in bed and watching the passers-by in this way, he will eventually slip into a dream while muttering something like 'Oh, I'm glad to see *him* out walking all the time again: he must have got over his sickness' or 'My goodness, look at that girl! She's really decked out today!'

In his student days, Sansaku had been terribly dissatisfied with the law as an academic discipline. Now he has the LLB attached to his name, but he still lives like a literature student, albeit one to whom current literature and literary people have come to seem just as dissatisfying and contemptible. Before, he (and perhaps only he) had believed that a literary man was someone who possessed keen powers of appreciation for all things in this world. Now, however, how did those literary people he had grown familiar with appear to him?

'To take an example close at hand,' thought Otsukotsu Sansaku, LLB, while observing the street from his closet bed as usual, 'the face of that woman passing by: among the writers I know' (and in fact, many of the literature-student friends he had while he was in law school were already well-known men of letters) 'is there even one who would be capable of composing a decent critique of how beautiful – or *not* beautiful – her face is, or her figure, or the way she wears her kimono, or her whole outfit?'

As a child, Sansaku tended to be smug and arrogant, always ready to show off his slightest ability. He was, in a word, vaguely contemptuous of just about everything and everyone. The tendency only increased with age to the point where now even he has come to find it somewhat abnormal. His sense of dissatisfaction has increased over the past two or three years such that all works of art – not only fiction but critical essays, dramatic texts, theatrical performances, paintings – are remarkable to him only for their innumerable shortcomings. He has come to feel that he is the only one who can perceive their flaws and virtues (if, indeed, they possess any virtues), that he alone truly understands them. He has gone so far as to think he should therefore provide models for other writers, write works that would serve to guide them to increasingly greater accomplishments; but in the end nothing has ever materialized.

Say, he goes out to eat, or to a performance of *gidayū*

or *rakugo* or *kōdan* or *naniwabushi*, or perhaps *ongyoku* or *buyō*, or down a notch to comic *teodori* or a *shinpa* tragedy: there is absolutely nothing about them that he does not know how to appreciate. He believes himself capable of discovering points of beauty in things that everyone else dismisses, and equally able to find bad points in things that everyone else admires, which makes him very pleased with himself.

'Had I become a sumo wrestler, I'm sure I would have numbered among the champions.' This was one of the more far-fetched thoughts that came to Sansaku one day as he was lying in his closet. 'Take that Ōarashi Tatsugorō, for example. Everybody is calling him unbeatable, but I knew him in middle school. At first, he and I were in the same class, but he was what they called a "backward" student and failed his exams twice in two years, ending up two grades behind me. Now you look at the sumo coverage in the paper and they're calling him an unusually smart wrestler. Well, I used to face him in judo all the time. I never had the physical strength, but my body was as unresisting as noodles, so the other guy could come at me with all his might, but I was like a willow in the wind – sure, it's an old figure of speech, but that's how I was – and nobody could ever knock me down. After a while, when the other guy started pressing, I'd see an opening and use his strength against him.

37

I always won. Old Ōarashi was fairly strong back then (though nothing special), but he never once beat me. If I had been training all this time like Ōarashi, I'd be great by now, or at least a damn good – if unusual – wrestler.'

The thought made Otsukotsu Sansaku feel he couldn't lose against Ōarashi even now. As he lay there in his closet imagining himself going up against each of the current sumo wrestlers, a big grin crossed his face.

'I wonder why I never put more of myself into studying the law,' thought Sansaku one day. 'I mean, think of that stiff-brained, tongue-tied, unimpressive-looking classmate of mine, Kakii: I see in today's paper they're calling him one of the up-and-coming hot young lawyers for some stupid case he's managed to win. The public is so damn easy to fool.' (Sansaku finds fault only with other people and forgets how hard the public is – and has been – for *him* to fool.) 'With my intelligence and my eloquence . . .' More than once, such thoughts inspired him to resolve to hit the law books and apply to be a judge or public prosecutor, but the inspiration never lasted more than an hour.

Ultimately, Sansaku lacked the most important elements for making a go of it in this world: perseverance, courage and common sense. To him, everything was 'stupid', everything was 'boring', everything he saw and heard filled him with displeasure and sometimes even anger. He was especially repulsed by his landlady's modern, swept-back hairstyle, to which she added an extra swirl by placing a black-lacquered wire frame against her scalp and covering it as best she could with her thinning hair, each strand stuck in place with pomade. She also appeared to spend her days in eager anticipation of being called 'Madam' not only by the maids but by her lodgers as well; she was trying to hide the fact that she was the mistress of an old country gentleman who visited her once or twice a week.

Only Sansaku made a point of calling her 'Mistress Proprietor', to which she never once deigned to reply. In spite of her refusal to respond, he would always ask her, 'How much fun are you getting out of life?'

'How much fun are you getting out of life?' was a pet phrase of Sansaku's.

'And you?' he once asked a friend. 'Are you enjoying life?'

The friend's only answer was a couple of non-committal grunts.

Another friend answered the question with a straight-out 'Not at all', to which Sansaku responded with his second pet phrase, 'Don't you want to die?'

'I'd like to be killed without knowing it,' the friend answered.

'Oh, oh, I can't take it any longer. I think I'll just find myself an aeroplane. I was one of the best gymnasts in middle school, so I'm sure I'd make a great pilot.' Sansaku's own special delusions of grandeur were taking flight. 'Too bad I don't have the one thing you really need for that . . . guts.' And soon he was drifting into his usual dream world in his closet bed.

Otsukotsu Sansaku had been an excellent long-jumper in middle school. He would take a twenty-foot run, plant his left foot on the line and sail into the air with his legs still rotating, as if swimming. As he neared the end of his jump, he would flip his body forwards, beginning a second arc and lengthening his distance, and then twist himself to make still another arc the moment before he touched down, forming three arcs in all. This way, he managed to jump much further than the other jumpers, who could only execute a single arc. Now, in his mind, he found himself using this technique to send his body aloft until he was sailing through the air without the aid of machinery. 'This is so much fun! And so easy for me! Oh, look! I'm flying over pine trees and all those people down there! Strange how no one seems amazed by this. But they'll realize it soon enough. I'll show them! They'll see how great my work is! Oh, I'm coming to the far bank of the river. But so what? River, ocean, they're all the same to me. Just go, go, it doesn't matter. See? It's nothing, I'm across the river now!' This was all in his dream, of course. He didn't know when he awoke, but the one thing he knew for sure was that the dream didn't end, as they so often did, in failure.

Otsukotsu Sansaku was not the least bit surprised when he opened his eyes. He really had been an excellent long-jumper at school, and he could clearly remember being able to propel his body further in mid-jump.

'Why haven't I tried that all this time? Sprinting to the line is the same as a plane accelerating for a take-off, and planting the foot is probably the take-off itself. Sure, that's it, I know I can do it! But . . .' Of course he started having second thoughts in the midst of his enthusiasm. 'But . . .' he thought to himself again.

He climbed out of his closet and gave it a try in his narrow six-mat room, but he could not even rise a foot above the tatami. In fact, he fell back so heavily and clumsily that he suspected he must have gained weight. 'No, I can't be this bad,' he told himself, his initial failure spurring him on to a more determined attempt. He stepped out into the corridor. Fortunately, there was no one present. It so happened that the house had undergone a major clean a month earlier, and a layer of oiled paper soaked with some kind of new chemical and varnish that had been put down to improve appearances and protect against bed bugs was still spread out over the floor. It was very slippery, and Sansaku enjoyed skating on it in his slippers whenever he was bored.

Now, using the aeronautical skills suggested by his dream, Sansaku gave himself over to running down the corridor and leaping through the air, but he could not make a tenth of the distance he used to cover at school. When he tried to plant his foot for the take-off on his fourth run down the corridor, he slipped and fell, slamming his shin against the banister and landing on his bottom. He was sitting there on the floor, scowling with pain, when the landlady with her hard-pomaded back-swept hairdo came climbing up the stairs.

'My goodness!' the woman cried with wide-open eyes. 'Mr Otsukotsu!'

'Madam!' Sansaku responded with the title he preferred not to use for her. He chose it because he had recalled something that made it necessary to call her 'Madam', something that even made him forget about the pain in his shin.

'Madam, I expect to receive a small payment tomorrow, so I will be able to . . .'

After he said this, he sighed from the pain in his leg and from the imagined consequences of his lie. Feeling a need for further words to cover his embarrassment, he came out with his habitual: 'Life is not much fun, is it, Madam?'

'Not much,' she replied resolutely. 'For either of us.'
Without so much as a smile, she headed back down the
stairs.

'Not for either of us, is it? I see, I see,' Otsukotsu Sansaku, LLB, still flat on his backside, mumbled to himself
as he watched her go.

General Kim

by Akutagawa Ryūnosuke

Their faces concealed by deep straw hats, two saffron-robed monks were walking down a country road one summer day in the village of Dong-u in the county of Ryonggang, in Korea's South P'yŏng'an Province. The pair were no ordinary mendicants, however. Indeed, they were none other than Katō Kiyomasa, lord of Higo, and Konishi Yukinaga, lord of Settsu, two powerful Japanese generals, who had crossed the sea to assess military conditions in the neighbouring kingdom of Korea.

The two trod the paths among the green paddy fields, observing their surroundings. Suddenly they came upon the sleeping figure of what appeared to be a farm boy, his head pillowed on a round stone. Kiyomasa studied the youth from beneath the low-hanging brim of his hat.

'I don't like the looks of this young knave.'

Without another word, the Demon General kicked the stone away. Instead of falling to earth, however, the young boy's head remained pillowed on the space the stone had occupied, its owner still sound asleep.

'Now I know for certain this is no ordinary boy,' Kiyomasa said. He grasped the hilt of the dagger hidden beneath his robe, thinking to nip this threat to his country in the bud. But Yukinaga, laughing derisively, held his hand in check.

'What can this mere stripling do to us? It is wrong to take life for no purpose.'

The two monks continued on down the path among the rice paddies, but the tiger-whiskered Demon General continued to look back at the boy from time to time . . .

Thirty years later, the men who had been disguised as monks back then, Kiyomasa and Yukinaga, invaded the eight provinces of Korea with a gigantic army. The people of the eight provinces, their houses set afire by the warriors from Wa (the 'Dwarf Kingdom', as they called Japan), fled in all directions, parents losing children, wives snatched from husbands. Hanseong had already fallen. Pyongyang was no longer a royal city. King Seonjo had barely managed to flee across the border to Ŭiju and now was anxiously waiting for the Chinese Ming Empire to send him reinforcements. If the people had merely stood by and let the forces of Wa run roughshod over them, they would have witnessed their eight beautiful provinces being transformed into one vast stretch of scorched earth. Fortunately, however, Heaven had not yet abandoned Korea. Which is to say that it entrusted the task of saving the country to Kim Eung-seo – the boy who had demonstrated his miraculous power on that path among the green paddy fields so long ago.

Kim Eung-seo hastened to the Tonggun Pavilion in Ŭiju, where he was allowed into the presence of His Majesty, King Seonjo, whose worn royal countenance revealed his utter exhaustion.

'Now that I am here,' Kim Eung-seo said, 'His Majesty may set his mind at ease.'

King Seonjo smiled sadly. 'They say that the Wa are stronger than demons. Bring me the head of a Wa general if you can.'

One of those Wa generals, Konishi Yukinaga, kept his longtime favourite *kisaeng*, Kye Wol-Hyang, in Pyongyang's Daedong Hall. None of the eight thousand other *kisaeng* was a match for her beauty. But just as she would never forget to put a jewelled pin in her hair each day, not one day passed in her service to the foreign general when Kye Wol-Hyang failed to grieve for her beloved country. Even when her eyes sparkled with laughter, a tinge of sadness showed beneath their long, dark lashes.

One winter night, Kye Wol-Hyang knelt by Yukinaga, pouring sake for him and his drinking companion, her pale, handsome elder brother. She kept pressing Yukinaga to drink, lavishing her charms on him with special warmth, for in the sake she had secreted a sleeping potion.

Once Yukinaga had drunk himself to sleep, Kye Wol-Hyang and her brother tiptoed out of the room. Yukinaga slept on in utter oblivion, his miraculous sword perched where he had left it on the rack outside the surrounding green-and-gold curtains. Nor was this entirely a matter of Yukinaga's carelessness. The small curtained area was known as a 'belled encampment'. If anyone were to attempt to enter the narrow enclosure, the surrounding bells would set up a noisy clanging that would rouse him. Yukinaga did not know, however, that Kye Wol-Hyang had stuffed the bells with cotton to keep them from ringing.

Kye Wol-Hyang and her brother came back into the room. Tonight she had concealed cooking ashes in the hem of her trailing embroidered robe. And her brother – no, this man with his sleeve pushed high up his bared arm was not in fact her brother but Kim Eung-seo, who, in pursuit of the king's orders, carried a long-handled Chinese green-dragon sword. They crept ever closer to the curtained enclosure when suddenly Yukinaga's

47

wondrous sword leaped from its scabbard as if it had sprouted wings and flew straight at General Kim. Unperturbed, General Kim launched a gob of spit at the sword, which seemed to lose its magic powers when smeared by the saliva and crashed to the floor.

With a huge cry, General Kim swung his green-dragon sword and lopped off the head of the fearsome Wa general. Fangs slashing in rage, the head struggled to reattach itself to the body. When she witnessed this stupefying sight, Kye Wol-Hyang reached into her robe and threw handfuls of ash on the haemorrhaging neck stump. The head leaped up again and again, but was unable to settle on to the ash-smeared wound.

Yukinaga's headless body, however, groped for its master's sword on the floor, picked it up and hurled it at General Kim. Taken by surprise, General Kim lifted Kye Wol-Hyang under one arm and jumped up to a high roof beam, but as it sailed through the air, Yukinaga's sword managed to slice off the vaulting General Kim's little toe.

Dawn had still not broken as General Kim, bearing Kye Wol-Hyang on his back, was running across a deserted plain. At the distant edge of the plain, the last traces of the moon were sinking behind a dark hill. At that moment General Kim recalled that Kye Wol-Hyang was pregnant. The child of a Wa general was no different from a poisonous viper. If he did not kill it now, there was no telling what evil it could foment. General Kim reached the same conclusion that Kiyomasa had arrived at thirty years earlier: he would have to kill the child.

Heroes have always been monsters who crushed sentimentalism underfoot. Without a moment's hesitation, General Kim killed Kye Wol-Hyang and ripped the child from her belly. In the fading moonlight the child was no more than a shapeless, gory lump, but it shuddered and raised a cry like that of a full-grown human being: 'If only you had waited three months longer, I would have avenged my father's death!'

As the voice reverberated across the dusky open field like the bellowing of a water buffalo, the last traces of the moon disappeared behind the hill.

Such is the story of the death of Konishi Yukinaga as it has been handed down in Korea. We know, of course, that Yukinaga did not lose his life in the Korean campaign. But Korea is not the only country to embellish its history. The history we Japanese teach our children – and our men, who are not much different from children – is full of such legends. When, for example, has a Japanese history textbook ever contained an account of a losing battle like this one from the *Nihon shoki* between the Chinese Tang and the Japanese Yamato?

The Tang general, leading 170 ships, made his camp at the Baekchon River. On the twenty-seventh day, the Yamato captain first arrived and fought with the Tang captain. Yamato could not win and retreated ... On the twenty-eighth day, the generals of Yamato ... leading the unorganized soldiers of Yamato's middle army ... advanced and attacked the Tang army at their fortified encampment. The Tang then came with ships on the left and right and surrounded them, and they fought. After a short time, the Yamato army had lost. Many went into the water and died. Their boats could also not be turned around.

To any nation's people, their history is glorious. The legend of General Kim is by no means the only one worth a laugh.